The Curious Case of the Missing Black Pawn

A Brooklyn Chess Story

Written and Illus-
trated by

Gabriel Puckett

Dedicated to my
Bensonhurst Chess
Club.

It was a chilly late October Friday at
Apple Rock Academy in Brooklyn,
New York. Caden was dreaming about
going to the mountains for the weekend.

The City is busy, and he wanted to be in the woods. Last summer he caught six salamanders with his grandpa. The last class of the day was chess, and then the weekend would start.

Mr. Puckett was Caden's chess teacher. He was really nice and really good at chess. The class was playing excitedly, and Caden was just about to get a checkmate! Caden loved chess, and not only was he in chess class, but he was also in Chess Club. Just as he was about to promote to a queen for the mate, Mr. Puckett said with a booming voice, "Scholars, when I say 'GO', silently reset your boards and put your pieces away two at a time. Make sure that you have ALL of your pieces be-fore you put them away."

Caden's partner quickly reached out her arm to shake Caden's hand. She was in a hurry to end the game before Caden could get the checkmate. In the process, she knocked over almost half of the chess pieces!

Class was almost over. Frustrated that

he didn't have time to finish the game,

Caden quickly picked up the pieces and

put them away. What he didn't notice

was that one black pawn was left on the

floor, alone and separated from his family.

The class exited the classroom for dismissal. Mr. Puckett packed up, turned off the lights, paused, took one final look at the room, and then left for the weekend. The only one left in the silent and dark classroom was the little black pawn. His name was Peshka.

Peshka had never been alone before. He had always either been in a chess bag packed in with his family and friends or on a board duking it out against his timeless opponents, the white pieces. It was time to be brave. Peshka knew that he had to get back into the bag somehow, some way. What he didn't know was that he was about to embark on the greatest adventure of his life.

Minutes turned into hours as Peshka tried to figure out how to get back onto the table and into the bag with his family. As the sun went down and the moon came up, the classroom started getting colder and colder. Someone had left the window open. Peshka spotted a chord going up to the air conditioning unit. If he could just climb up the chord and get onto the windowsill, he might

be able to leap onto the table and make it back into the bag.

He began to climb. There were times when he thought he wouldn't be able to hold onto the chord any longer, but finally he made it to the windowsill. Sighing in relief and gasping for air, he was almost home. Peshka knew that if he took a running leap he might be able to make it to the table. It couldn't be any harder than jumping two spaces which he had done hundreds of times as an opening move on the chess board. Peshka backed up toward the open window to get as much running space as possible. It was freezing up here, and the wind was blowing **hard**. He took one more step toward the open window to get a little bit more running space. It was one step too far. The wind blew and sucked him right out the window. Peshka plummeted five stories. His heart and his hopes of being reunited with his family plummeted with him. It felt like

he was falling forever..

and ever..

and ever!

An eternity later, he hit the ground - and bounced!

Peshka landed in the grass. He was ok, but how was he ever going to get back into school? It was late. He was cold and alone. Suddenly he heard something moving through the grass behind him. He turned around, peering through the tall grass. He saw two big, glowing yellow eyes staring right back at him.

It was the biggest alley cat he had

ever seen, jet black, crouched, and

ready to pounce. His stomach dropped.

The cat leaped. Peshka dashed between

her legs. He could see the cat's ribs. It

looked like she hadn't had a meal in days.

He hit the sidewalk and kept running, hearing the cat hiss in frustration at having missed her prey. Suddenly the ground disappeared from under-

neath Peshka again as he fell into the gutter and splattered into a pile of stinky mush. He had fallen into the sewer. He was safe from the cat, but it smelled really bad in here, and he was even further from home. He looked out of the gutter and saw the full moon shining above the city. Wondering if he would ever make it home, he found an old sock and made a bed for the night.

That night Peshka awoke to the
sound of whistling and saw what looked
like a little sea captain floating by on a
tiny ship, or maybe it was just a dream.
He dreamed about being back with his

family. He dreamed about playing chess in the classroom with the sun shining through the window, getting promoted, and winning the game for black. It was a sweet dream, but it lasted only a short time as he was awakened to the sound of scurrying nearby.

"What do we have here!?" asked a raspy and mean voice. Peshka opened his eyes and saw a huge rat standing over him. He had an eye patch and looked like he had been in more than one scuffle in his days. He was missing

a piece of his ear and had a hook instead

of a paw. Two other rats were with him.

Peshka was surrounded. The one with

the patch was obviously the leader.

"What on earth is it!?" exclaimed the

leader, towering over Peshka. When he

spoke, he took a bite of a chicken wing,

and spit came flying out of his mouth,

landing on Peshka's head.

"It looks like some kind of weird insect," said the pale white rat standing behind Peshka, "like an ant without legs." Its eyes were red and unsettling.

"It's bald!" said a fat rat, poking Peshka with a chicken bone in the head. The rats had a laugh.

Peshka mustered up some courage and in a shaky voice said, "My name is Peshka. I'm a chess piece."

"A chess what?" asked the leader. "What is chess?"

"Chess is a game that makes people smart. That's probably why you don't know about it."

The other rats burst out laughing, and the leader got furious! He took his chicken wing and smacked the closest rat in the head with it, knocking the rat over and creating a commotion. Peshka knew that these rats were trouble. He saw this as his chance to escape. He took off running. The leader caught him with his hook. "We're not done with you yet, little chess piece," said the lead rat with a crooked grin. "Were gonna make you walk the plank." The rest of the rats snickered in agreement.

They marched Peshka through endless tunnels and corridors in the pitch black sewer, miles beneath the streets of bustling Brooklyn. Eventually they reached the edge of a waterfall that fell into nothing. The smell was terrible. He couldn't see the bottom. They walked him to the edge of the waterfall where there was a stick poking out over the edge. "Walk the plank!" ordered the white rat, poking him with a toothpick from behind. Peshka didn't see any way out. He was surrounded, and the only place he could go was out onto the rickety old stick over nothingness. He took one step out and stopped.

"WALK!" yelled all the rats in unison.

Suddenly Peshka heard whistling. It was the same whistling he had heard the night before! It hadn't been a

dream! Out of the darkness came sailing

a tiny, chunky mouse riding on an apple

core with a sail made out of an old nap-

kin!

The mouse had a sea captain's hat on. He yelled, "Land a'hoy!" His apple core ship crashed onto the shore and sent all of the rats plunging over the waterfall into the abyss!

Only Peshka was spared because he had been standing on the plank. They heard three consecutive kerplunks as the rats hit the water and then scurried off into the pitch black, arguing and scuffling what seemed like miles beneath them.

"The name's Squeek," said the chunky mouse, putting out his hand to shake Peshka's.

"I'm Peshka. Thanks for rescuing me! I thought I was a goner!"

"No problem," said the mouse. "Those rats are always causing trouble around here. I can't stand bullies, so I don't put up with them." "Where are you from?" Squeek asked.

Suddenly Peshka realized how far he was from home. It felt like forever since he had left the classroom, and he had had too many adventures for one little pawn to handle. The tears started to bubble up, and Peshka started to sob. He told Squeek everything - about the chess game, the window, the cat, and the rats. Sniffling and with big crocodile tears in his eyes, he looked at Squeek and said, "I just wanna go home."

Squeek looked at him with kind eyes and patted him on the back. "Chin up, little buddy. I know where your school is! I know everything about Brooklyn, and I know these sewers like the back of my hand. I can get you back home!"

"Really!?" exclaimed Peshka. "That would be amazing!" He felt some hope returning to his bones. They hopped on the apple core ship and set sail. As they talked, he realized it had been two days since he had left the classroom. It was impossible to keep track of time in the sewer because he couldn't see the sun. The two days had felt like a lifetime.

At last they reached the gutter where Peshka had first fallen into the sewer. The sun was pouring through, and it was hard for Peshka to see. He had been in the dark so long. Squeek said that he had to go. Peshka had no doubt that Squeek was off on another adventure. He seemed to live and breath adventure. Peshka, on the other hand, was ready to be safe and sound in his warm chess bag with his family. He was ready to be home. He thanked Squeek for his friendship and help. The two parted ways.

Peshka stepped out into the street. It was a chilly and breezy day, but the sun felt good and warm. He breathed a sigh of relief. The air was fresh. He was almost home. He could see the window that he had fallen out of. He started to walk toward the school. No one would believe the adventure that he had been on! Wow, were they going to be happy to see him! Suddenly he heard a hissing behind him.

Peshka whipped around to see the crusty old black alley cat crouched and ready to pounce. Her eyes were locked on him with the singular focus of a perfect predator. Her ribs were showing more than ever which told him that she hadn't eaten since their last meeting. Her teeth looked way too sharp as she hissed and walked toward him. He knew that he would never be able to outrun her. He turned to try.

As he took his first step, Peshka felt

a huge paw pummel him onto the side-

walk. Lying in darkness under the paw

of his feline attacker, Peshka lay motionless. He wondered if he would ever see his family again.

Then he heard a voice. "Shoo cat! Get out of here!!" It was a familiar voice. He heard footsteps running toward him. The paw lifted and vanished almost as quickly as it had appeared. Dizzy from being knocked into the sidewalk, Peshka looked up and saw … Caden!! Caden and his big sister Kaylee were both running toward him. They were both in Chess Club, so Peshka knew that he was saved. "Look what I found!" yelled Caden to his mom and dad.

Caden was holding a jar with seven salamanders in it. They had gotten back from the mountains just in time to res-

cue Peshka from the deadly feline. Relief flooded Peshka. He knew he was in
good hands. Caden's mom laughed and
said, "Wow! Mr. Puckett is going to be
happy to see this little guy!" They all
looked up at the window where the
chess room was.

"Wow! I wonder how he got out?"
said Kaylee.

"If you only knew," thought Peshka
to himself.

The next day was Monday. In the morning, Kaylee and Caden dropped Peshka off with Mr. Puckett. Mr. Puckett was so thankful to see his pawn. He thanked Kaylee and Caden and sent them on their way with a prize from the treasure chest. As Mr. Puckett walked with the pawn to put it back in the bag, he took one last look at it. It was almost like he knew that Peshka had been up to some kind of mischief and adventure.

"How could he know?" wondered

Peshka.

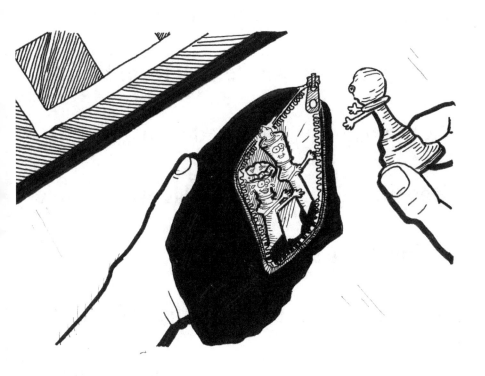

Mr. Puckett zipped Peshka back

into the chess bag. His family and

friends were thrilled to see him! They hugged him as he burst out telling them about all of the crazy adventures he had been on. As he was telling them his story, the bag was unzipped above him. It was time for chess club! He would have to finish his story later.

Peshka never forgot that weekend. Caden ended up winning the game and getting a checkmate with Peshka. Peshka was a hero! It was a glorious way to end an amazing adventure. In one

weekend, the little black pawn had gone

from the gutter to the chess board and

won the game for black.

It was an adventure he would never

forget and a day that would live on in

the silent history of chess pieces at Apple Rock Academy forever.

Every chess piece is important, and just because a piece is small doesn't mean that it can't make a big difference. Peshka learned something that day. He learned that even though he is a very small pawn in a very big world, he can still make a very big difference.

Take care of your chess pieces because you never know what happens in the curious world of chess pieces when no one is looking. Even a little pawn

can make a big, big difference!

The End

Pawn Rules

"Hi kids! I'm Professor Pawn! I am going to explain to you all of the pawn rules. Follow me to success on the board!"

White pawns start on the 2nd rank and black pawns start on the 7th rank. The white pawns want to go to the 8th Rank and the black pawns want to make it to the 1st rank. Remember, white goes first!

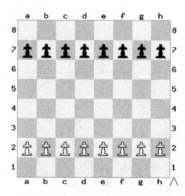

Pawns move forward and capture on diagonals. They never move backwards or sideways. This white pawn could capture the knight or the rook. It cannot capture the bishop because pawns only capture on diagonals moving forward.

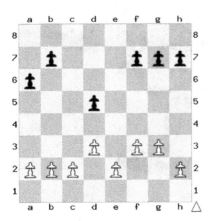

Pawns are strongest together, an isolated pawn is a sad pawn. It is more vulnerable to attack. White could easily capture the black pawn on d5 because no other black pawns are backing it up. White could also stop the d5 pawn's advance by placing an outpost piece such as a knight on d4.

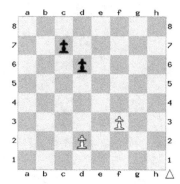

The first time a pawn moves, it may jump two spaces. The white pawn on d2 could hop to d4. The black pawn on c7 could hop to c5. However, the white pawn on f3 and black pawn on d6 can only move one space because they have already moved.

Promotion: When a pawn gets to the other side, it may "promote" to any piece it likes except for a pawn or a king. It can turn into a bishop, rook, knight, or queen. Think of it kind of like a graduation. The pawn worked very hard to get across the board and nOw it's getting "promoted"!

En Passant:

En Passant is the weirdest rule in all of chess. It's the only rule where a piece can be captured on a square that it's not even on. It's almost like the piece gets abducted by martians! It just gets snatched up. Read on to discover where "en passant" came from, why it exists, and how you can do it to your next opponent..

"En Passant" is French for "In Passing". Once upon a time, over 400 years ago, (thats the last time a rule was added to the game of chess) pawns only moved one space at a time. Chess was a great game but it took a long time for the pawns to get into the action. People were getting bored and they wanted the game to start quick. So they invented a rule which said that the first time a pawn moves it can jump two spaces. This was great! Now the action could get started right away! However, there was a little predicament. If the pawn jumped two spaces at a time he could potentially escape the enemies attacking pawns on the neighboring files. This didn't seem fair. So the chess authorities decided to make a rule, and get ready for this, because it is the weirdest rule in all of chess. They decided that if a pawn jumps two spaces over a square that is under attack by an enemy pawn, the enemy may capture it and land on the square that the pawn jumped over. This is the only rule in all of chess where a piece gets captured on a square that it's not even on! In order to do "en passant" the opponent has to capture on the first move after the pawn has jumped two spaces. If he/she waits, then the opportunity for "en passant" has passed. Weird rule right!? Peshka thinks so too, but it sure does make the game more exciting!

Here is an example. It's blacks turn. If black chose to jump two spaces and move the f7 pawn to f5, white could use "en passant". The white e5 pawn would capture diagonally and land on f6 successfully capturing the black pawn on the square that it just jumped over. It's almost like a magic trick. It's important to be aware of this rule because someday someone might try to do it to you.

"Now that you know 'en passant' and the rest of the pawn rules you are ready to start your adventure into the world of chess! Good luck on your journey and may the pawns be forever in your favor!"

-Professor Pawn

CPSIA information can be obtained
at www.ICGtesting.com
Printed in the USA
BVHW041504290419
546834BV00028B/2201/P

9 781733 921206